Tickling Tigers

Sean Taylor   Jo Brown

Sandy Creek

Tigers are big and tigers are scary.
Tigers are quick and tigers are hairy.
We climb, we growl, we jump, we chew...
and we're terribly good at tickling too.

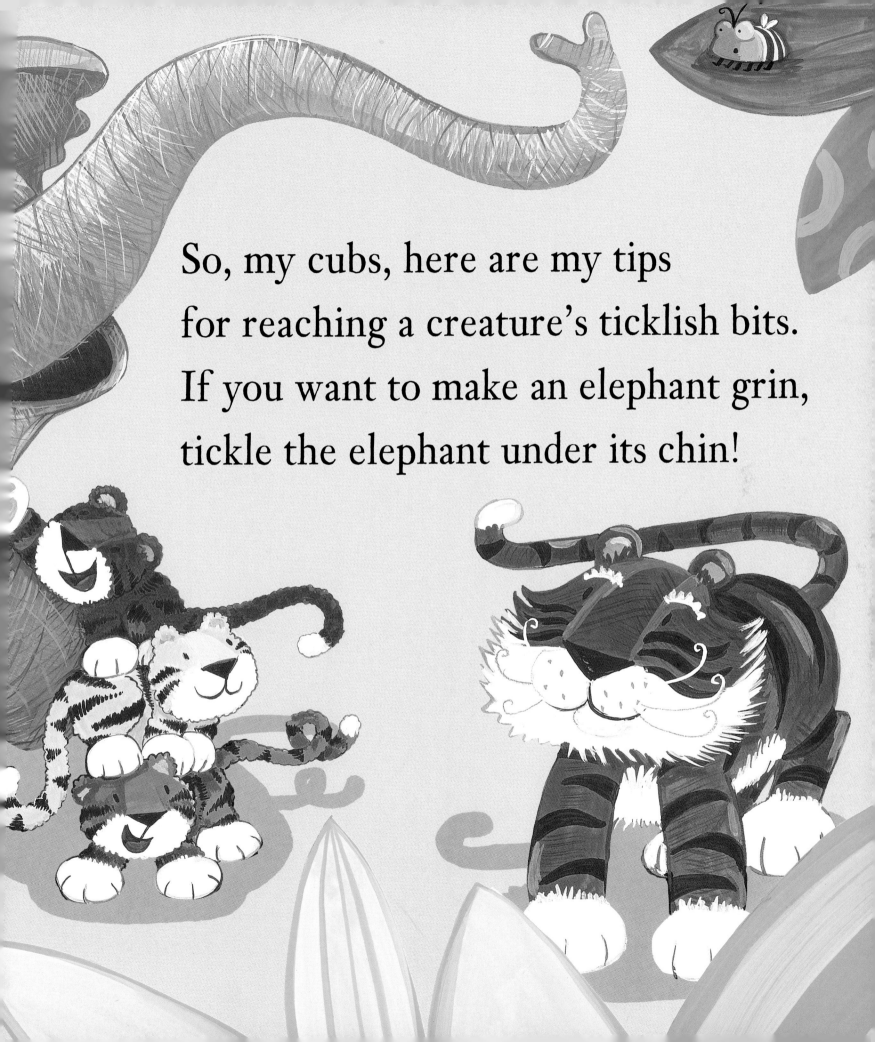

So, my cubs, here are my tips
for reaching a creature's ticklish bits.
If you want to make an elephant grin,
tickle the elephant under its chin!

You think that tickling a frog could be funny?
You're right! Try tickling it on its tummy!

To tickle a crocodile, everyone knows,
you find a feather and tickle its nose!

You'll get a giraffe to giggle with glee
if you tickle it lightly behind the knee!

With a gorilla you stay very calm . . .

. . . then tickle it quickly under each arm!

And tickling small tigers
is easy, you know.
You just have to
tickle them
from top
to toe!

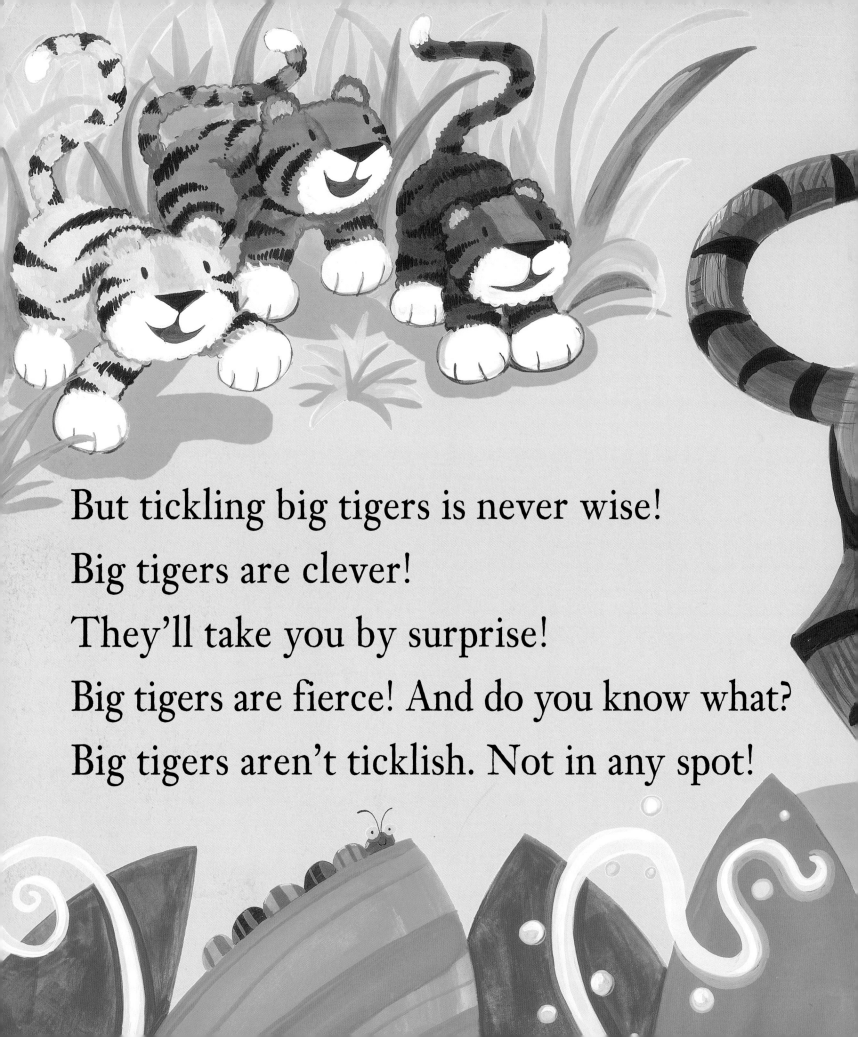

But tickling big tigers is never wise!

Big tigers are clever!

They'll take you by surprise!

Big tigers are fierce! And do you know what?

Big tigers aren't ticklish. Not in any spot!

Except for **me!** The tiniest tickle makes me jiggle and giggle and wriggle!

Yes, you see, that's how it's done,
my stripy little bundles of fun.
And there's nothing in the world more snug
than a just-tickled-tiger hug!

For all children who've never
been tickled by a tiger
S.T.

For my two darlings,
Christian and Zazie
J.B.

This 2010 edition published by Sandy Creek
by arrangement with Orchard Books

Sandy Creek
122 Fifth Avenue
New York, NY 10011

ISBN: 978 1 4351 2841 5

A CIP catalogue record for this book is available from the British Library.

Printed and bound in China
Manufactured April/2010

Lot 1 3 5 7 9 10 8 6 4 2